THE FIRST BLADE OF SWEETGRASS

THE FIRST BLADE OF SWEETGRASS

A Native American Story

Story by
Suzanne Greenlaw
and Gabriel Frey

Illustrations by
Nancy Baker

TILBURY HOUSE PUBLISHERS

As Grandmother's blue truck crested the hill, Musqon saw the ocean for the first time that day. The water's surface sparkled in the sunlight. "Look, Uhkomi. Is this where we pick sweetgrass?" Musqon asked excitedly.

"Yes, Musqon," Grandmother said. "Sweetgrass grows in the salt marsh, where the river meets the ocean.

"My grandmother brought me here when I was a girl. She was my first sweetgrass teacher. Every summer I would help her pick sweetgrass to weave into her baskets.

"Our people have been coming here to pick sweetgrass for generations. We call it welimahaskil, and we use it in ceremony as well as baskets. Sweetgrass is a spiritual medicine for us."

Walking into the marsh, Musqon saw the grass dance with the wind. All the grasses shone bright against the sun. "Uhkomi, how will I tell which grass is sweetgrass?" she asked. "All the grass looks the same."

"I'll show you, Tus," said Grandmother, "but then you must try to find it on your own while I pick enough sweetgrass for the baskets I will sell next summer."

Grandmother stopped
in the shade of a tree
and put down their bag.

"This is where we'll pick," she said. "It's important to remember that we never pick the first blade of sweetgrass we see. If we never pick the first blade, we will never pick the last one. We must make sure there will be sweetgrass here for the next generation."

"Come here, Tus," Grandmother said. "Bend down and look at the grasses closely. Sweetgrass has a shiny green tassel and blades and a purple stem, and it gives itself to you. If you tug lightly on a piece of sweetgrass, it will let go. If you have to pull hard, you are not pulling sweetgrass."

"I see it, Uhkomi," Musqon said confidently.

"I know how to pick sweetgrass."

Musqon got down on her knees and was enveloped by grass. She could see her grandmother's head through the tips of the tall grass. The air felt cooler close to the ground, and the thin whine of mosquitoes grew distant.

Musqon looked for the purple-stemmed sweetgrass, but all the grasses looked the same. Frustrated, she started to pull at any stems she could reach. Some broke off where she tugged. Others pulled out of the soil.

Musqon stood up with a handful of grass.

"Uhkomi, look at all the sweetgrass I picked," she said.

Grandmother smiled. "Tus, that is a good first try, but that's not sweetgrass. I'll show you again."

She knelt beside Musqon and said, "First you have to look at the different grasses and get to know them."

"Do you see this grass
with a thick stalk and
a light-green color?
That's not sweetgrass.

"This plant has a small
white flower. That's not
sweetgrass either.

"Sweetgrass is a shiny
emerald-green with a
purple bottom."

"Sit here and take your time. Your ancestors are here with you.
My grandmother is here with you, helping you."

Musqon sat in the cool air and watched the colors of the grass shift with the wind. A large bird flew into the marsh, then glided onto the water. She looked at her grandmother and saw that she had already picked a lot of sweetgrass. Musqon closed her eyes and thought about her grandmother as a little girl in this very same place.

She thought about her ancestors here in the marsh. Slowly the smell of sweetgrass drifted by her. It was the same sweet hay smell that was in her grandmother's basket room. Musqon opened her eyes and smiled. In the distance she could see her ancestors picking sweetgrass in the marsh with her.

She looked down at the grasses again. The beautiful emerald green color of sweetgrass popped out from all the other grasses. She could see it! Musqon reached eagerly to pick the first blade of sweetgrass she saw, but then stopped.

Remembering her grandmother's words, Musqon reached past the first blade of sweetgrass and tugged lightly on the next one. She felt the roots let go of the soil as the grass gave itself to her hand.

"Look, Uhkomi, I have sweetgrass!" Musqon exclaimed.

"Kuli-kiseht, Tus. That's right!" Grandmother said. "Next I will teach you how to braid sweetgrass for baskets."

Musqon picked while catspaws of wind chased each other in darker fans on the blue bay.

She was excited to get home and show her parents all the sweetgrass she had picked.

Perhaps next summer she could teach her younger sister, Alamossit, how to pick sweetgrass.

A Note from Suzanne and Gabriel

The Wabanaki Confederacy—the People of First Light—comprises the Maliseet, Mi'kmaq, Abenaki, Passamaquoddy, and Penobscot nations. Our territories once covered present-day Maine, parts of Quebec, and the Maritime Provinces of Canada. Though our lands are much reduced today, the Wabanaki remain a thriving and vibrant community.

Sweetgrass (*Hierochole ordorata*) is a perennial grass that grows in rhizomatous mats (that is, by means of horizontally spreading rootstalks) in salt marshes and freshwater meadows in the northern United States, southern Canada, and northern Europe. The sweetly scented, emerald-green grass holds spiritual, economic,  and cultural importance for the Wabanaki and many other First Nations across the continent.

It is used in smudging ceremonies, a spiritual practice among Native peoples. It is also used as a ceremonial gift and is woven into baskets.

The sweetgrass baskets sold in coastal tourist communities by Wabanaki basket makers starting in the 1800s were referred to as "fancy baskets" due to their elaborate weaves and designs. Sales of these baskets—typically woven with finely braided sweetgrass on a base of black ash—often provided a large portion of a family's yearly income.

Through thousands of years of harvesting sweetgrass, the Wabanaki have accumulated extensive knowledge of sweetgrass ecology, habitat, and stewardship practices. We know that selectively harvesting sweetgrass promotes new growth. In return the sweetgrass provides spiritual medicine, a sense of identity, and an avenue of connection with a landscape and our ancestors. Wabanaki people practice traditional sweetgrass harvesting methods in the same locations where our ancestors harvested before us.

Passamaquoddy-Maliseet Words

Uhkomi: grandmother

Musqon: blue sky

Alamossit: hummingbird

Kuli-kiseht: good job

Tus: daughter (term of endearment)

Welimahaskil: sweetgrass

For a dictionary of Passamaquoddy-Maliseet words and their pronunciations, see the Passamaquoddy-Maliseet Language Portal, https://pmportal.org. There you can translate words to and from English and hear the Passamaquoddy-Maliseet words spoken.

Hardcover ISBN 978-0-88448-760-9 • Tilbury House Publishers • Thomaston, Maine • www.tilburyhouse.com

Library of Congress Control Number: 2021935470

Designed by Frame25 Productions • Printed in China • 10 9 8 7 6 5 4 3 2 1

Suzanne

Suzanne and Gabriel with Musqon

Gabriel

Suzanne Greenlaw is a citizen of the Houlton Band of Maliseet Indians. A Ph.D. candidate in the School of Forest Resources at the University of Maine, she works to restore Wabanaki stewardship practices throughout Maine. **Gabriel Frey** (pronounced Fray) is a citizen of the Passamaquoddy Nation. He is an awarded-winning basket maker, artist, and cultural knowledge keeper. His mother and Suzanne and Gabriel's two daughters, Musqon and Alamossit, helped inspire this story.

Nancy Baker is a Maine artist, illustrator, and muralist whose landscapes, still lifes, and figurative works in oils and pastels are represented by Mars Hall Gallery in Tenants Harbor, Maine. While visiting the sweetgrass meadows of Mount Desert Island and Acadia National Park with Suzanne and Gabriel, Nancy learned the ecology and cultural importance of sweetgrass and witnessed the majesty of the landscape in which it grows, qualities that she has worked to convey in these illustrations.

Tilbury House is the publisher of Native American picture book stories including:

Kunu's Basket: A Story for Indian Island
978-0-88448-461-5
Lee DeCora Francis
Illustrated by Susan Drucker

Thanks to the Animals
978-0-88448-753-1
Allen Sockabasin
Illustrated by Rebekah Raye

Muskrat Will Be Swimming
978-0-88448-280-2
Cheryl Savageau
Illustrated by Robert Hynes

A Caribou Alphabet
978-0-88448-446-2
Mary Beth Owens

Visit us at www.tilburyhouse.com.